'The Snowman Who Di

by Jerzy Jon

MW00946651

Illustrations: alistebals

Links to FREE material:- get your parents to click on or type the link(s) below into a computer and leave a name and email to receive the free gifts.

FREE Audiobook

https://myfreebookgift.com/107/snowman_who_did_not_want _to_melt/index.html

FREE Colouring Pages

https://myfreebookgift.com/107/snowman_who_did_not_want _to_melt_2/index.html

To find out where the Hidden Snowmen are

https://myfreebookgift.com/107/snowman_who_did_not_want_to_ melt_3/index.html

This book is for my great nieces and great nephews and grandson

'The Snowman Who Didn't Want to MELT'

by Jerzy Jones

'Come on, Alex, put his nose on.' Olivia shouted to her younger brother excitedly, pleased the snowman was almost finished.

Three of them - Dad, Olivia and Alex - had spent the afternoon building him.

Dad picked up Alex to put the carrot nose on the snowman's face then they danced around the snowman, singing,

'WE'VE BUILT A SNOWMAN!

WE'VE BUILT A SNOWMAN!'

That night, Olivia couldn't get to sleep because she was so excited there was a snowman in her garden. All she wanted to do was go down and keep him company.

About to drop off, Olivia heard a CRASHING noise outside. She got up and peeped through the curtains, shutting them quickly, her mouth wide open in amazement.

She peeped through the curtains again and saw the same thing.

The Snowman was waving up at her.

Quickly, she put on her dressing gown and went into her brother's bedroom. With a finger pressed to her lips, she gently shook him awake, whispering, 'Come with me.'

The children crept downstairs.

'Where we going?' Alex said.

'You'll see,' Olivia said.

The Snowman met them by the back door. He was almost crying.

'What's the matter?' Olivia asked.

'I'm starting to melt and I don't want to,' the Snowman said. 'Look.' He lifted his left hand which had partly disappeared, tears coming to his eyes.

'We'll help you,' Alex said, after getting over the shock of seeing a living snowman.

'Mam's got an old fridge-freezer in the garage she doesn't use,' said Olivia, 'we can put you in there for the night.'

Alex scooped up a handful of snow as they went.

The Snowman followed the children out to the garage. Olivia opened the fridge-freezer for him to step in.

'This is much better. Thank you. I'm feeling colder already, and happier,' the Snowman said.

'Wait,' Alex said, 'let's fix your hand.' He used the snow he'd scraped up to make the Snowman's hand whole again.

The next morning, after breakfast, the children rushed to the garage and opened the fridge–freezer.

The Snowman was sleeping, snoring loudly.

'ZZZ…zzz! ZZZ…zzz!'

'Let's leave him until we find a better place for him to live,' Olivia said.

Alex nodded, agreeing with her, and closed the fridge-freezer door.

'Where we going to take him then?' Alex said.

'We need somewhere that's quiet, where nobody goes,' Olivia said.

. 'And cold.' Alex said.

'Yes, and cold.' Olivia said.

'Why can't he stay here?' Alex asked.

'Because he's cramped in there. I'm surprised he's still fast asleep.' Olivia said, checking on the Snowman, again.

'ZZZ...zzz! ZZZ...zzz!'

There was silence as the two children thought long and hard about where they could find a new home for the Snowman.

Suddenly, they called out together, 'Mr. Jones! The Butcher.' They laughed at having the same idea at the same time.

'Remember what he said after we warned him about the fire in his shop?' Olivia said.

They both repeated what Mr. Jones had said to them last year. 'If there's anything I can do to help you, just let me know.'

They ran off to see Mr. Jones and explained about the Snowman.

'You bring him round here whenever you're ready,' Mr. Jones said. 'I've got a nice quiet place for him at the back of my meat freezer.'

'We'll have to be careful,' Olivia said, 'walking down the street with a Snowman will stop the traffic.'

Mr. Jones wasn't sure what to believe but said, 'Don't worry I'll wait here until you arrive.'

'Thank you, Mr. Jones,' the children said as they skipped, happily, out of the butcher's shop.

Later that afternoon the children slinked out of the house and into the garage.

The Snowman smiled when he saw them. 'I was worried you'd forgotten about me,' he said.

'We'll never forget you,' Alex said. 'We've found a place for you to live.'

'For Me? Really?' The Snowman beamed with delight.

'Yes. Come on,' Olivia said, 'Mr. Jones is waiting for us.'

Olivia, Alex and Mr. Snowman sneaked down the road, hiding behind bushes whenever people and cars passed, as they made their way to what, they hoped, would be the Snowman's new home.

When they arrived, the butcher's shop was empty and the lights were out.

Olivia knocked on the door, a worried look on her face.

At last, Mr. Jones opened the door and…

……………………………………………..

FAINTED.

The children rushed to help him.

'I'm sorry children and Mr....Mr Snow...Snowman,' Mr. Jones said, when he came round, staring, wide eyed, at the living Snowman standing in front of him. 'I never believed it.'

'Does this mean you haven't got a new home for him?' Olivia asked, with a sad expression on her face.

Mr. Jones, now smiling, said, 'Of course I have a home for him.'

He got up. 'Follow me.'

Mr. Jones took them out to the back garden and unlocked a big old shed. 'Come on in,' he said to the three of them.

'Mr. Snowman, you can stay here for as long as you want.' Mr. Jones said.

'Can I really?' The Snowman said, surprised. 'This is perfect. And nice and cold.'

The children and Mr. Jones shivered.

'This will be your new home and you children can visit whenever you like. I'll give you a key each so you can let yourselves in and out.' Mr. Jones said.

Grinning happily, the three friends thanked Mr. Jones and they all hi-fived.

Talking points and optional exercises for Teachers and Parents

- Talk about the picture on the front cover. Can the children guess what the book is about?

- How did they think the story was going to end after the first read? Were they right? Discuss other story endings.

- Why do you think the Butcher didn't believe the children?

- See if the children can take turns to read the story aloud. Remember to praise the children for their effort to read the book and don't forget to help with difficult words.

- What will Olivia and Alex do when they visit the Snowman? List or draw some ideas. - eg. Play games, chat about his new home.

- Make a model of the Snowman with cotton wool, cardboard or other materials. Ask the children to draw the story characters.

Did the children find the little snowmen hidden in each of the drawings? Ask them to look for them and point them out (14 in total). If they can't find the hidden snowmen type or copy the link below into a computer. Leave your name and email address to receive a page identifying where the hidden snowmen are located.

https://myfreebookgift.com/107/snowman_who_did_not_want_to_melt_3/index.html

Follow the author via the following link:-

https://amazon.com/author/jerzyjones

Acknowledgements: Extreme gratitude to all who supported me in this project including early readers, Sara Lindsey Hayes, Samuel Harris and Sarah Kim Harris.

Check out other books by author Jerzy Jones: No.1 best seller – 'Corbus Saves his Friends'

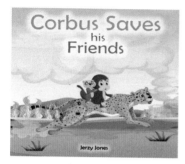

Description – Corbus the Cheetah's speed can cause havoc but it also comes to the rescue to save his friends when danger sweeps across the land.

UK Link   www.amazon.co.uk/dp/B08JPYN7WX

USA Link https://amzn.to/34CsZ5s

No.1 New release in the US – 'The FREEZING Cold Snowman'

Description – Two brothers build a snowman in the garden. At night the snowman feels the cold and comes Tap Tap Tapping the window looking for warmth. Find out how the brothers react to this unusual but magical happening.

UK Link   www.amazon.co.uk/dp/B08MV5TBSK

USA Link https://amazon.com/dp/B08MV5TBSK

I'd be really grateful if you'd leave an honest review on Amazon if you read any of my books – personal request from Jerzy Jones

Made in the USA
Middletown, DE
15 January 2024

47874502R00018